Y0-CBH-796

Be Still!

The Story of a Little Bird and
How He Found His Purpose

written and illustrated by
Debbie Mackall

ISBN 0-9762273-0-4

Mackall, Debbie 1958 –
Be Still/Debbie Mackall

10 9 8 7 6 5 4 3 2 1

Published by Dimensions in Media, Inc.
Printed in the USA.

© 2004 Dimensions in Media, Inc.
All rights reserved. No part of this book may be reproduced or transmitted in any form or by any means, electronic or mechanical, including photocopying, recording, or by any information storage and retrieval system, without the written permission of the Publisher.

Telephone: 847-726-2093
Email: debbie@dimensionsinmedia.com

For all of those who are looking
for their purpose.

Special thanks to Mom and Dad for their ongoing support,
and Greg, for his patient, willing, hard work helping me with the
nuts and bolts parts of the operation.

Thanks to Luis for helping to motivate me, and all of my
friends for their loyalty and encouragement.

Thanks to Cheryl Chaffin for her input and teachings.

Thank you to Maggie for your support and enthusiasm,
to David for your ideas and energy.
Thanks to Betsy for your hard work and support of me and my projects.
And to Sandy for always being there for me.

Thank you to Gurumayi
for showing me how to Be Still.

In gratitude to these people who helped make this book a reality.

I love you!

Someone once said to Rumi,

"If you believe in silence,

why have you done nothing but talk and talk

and write and sing and dance?"

He laughed and said,

"The radiant one inside me has

never said a word."

This is a story about a little bird who lives near a lake behind a cozy cottage.

One summer day Little Bird woke up after a long sleep. He had been dreaming about many special creatures: fireflies who could light up the sky, elephants who could spray water through their long noses and giraffes with long necks who could reach high into a tree without leaving the ground.

"How can I find out what is special about me?" he asked his mother.

"Be still!" said Mother Bird, who was trying to clean the birdhouse.

"She's too busy," thought the little bird.

So he flew off to the park to look for something to make him special.

Little Bird saw a squirrel gathering acorns. He knew Mr. Squirrel was collecting food for his family.

He flew over and said, "Mr. Squirrel, I want to be special. Should I be gathering acorns? What should I do?"

The squirrel was very surprised to be bothered by such questions.
He looked the little bird
right in the eye
and exclaimed,

"Be still!"

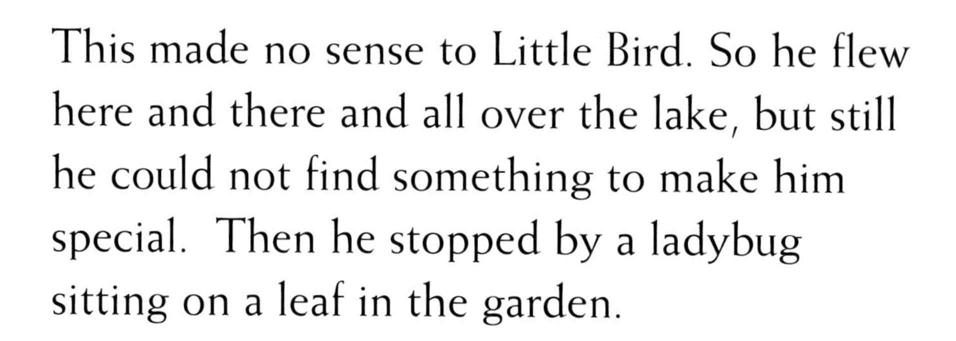

This made no sense to Little Bird. So he flew here and there and all over the lake, but still he could not find something to make him special. Then he stopped by a ladybug sitting on a leaf in the garden.

"I'm looking for something to make me special." he told her. "Do you know what I should do?"

"Be still!" I'm busy," exclaimed the ladybug, turning to nibble on her lunch.

"Why won't anyone answer my question?" wondered the little bird. He flew down to the shore where he saw two swans swimming gracefully in the water. They were so lovely it was obvious they were special. He thought maybe they would help.

Little Bird asked them, "I want to be special. Should I swim like you? What should I do?"

"Be still!" said the swans as they swam away together.

Little Bird began to wonder if all the animals were just saying this because they did not want him around. He started to fly away when he heard a splash behind him.

A big brown turtle had just climbed onto the shore for a nap. He found a cozy place near the flowers to sit and with his big sleepy eyes looked at Little Bird.

"I want to find something to make me special!" the little bird told the turtle.

"I've looked everywhere and asked everyone. Can you help me turtle?"

"Be still!" exclaimed the turtle closing his eyes as he dozed off in the sun.

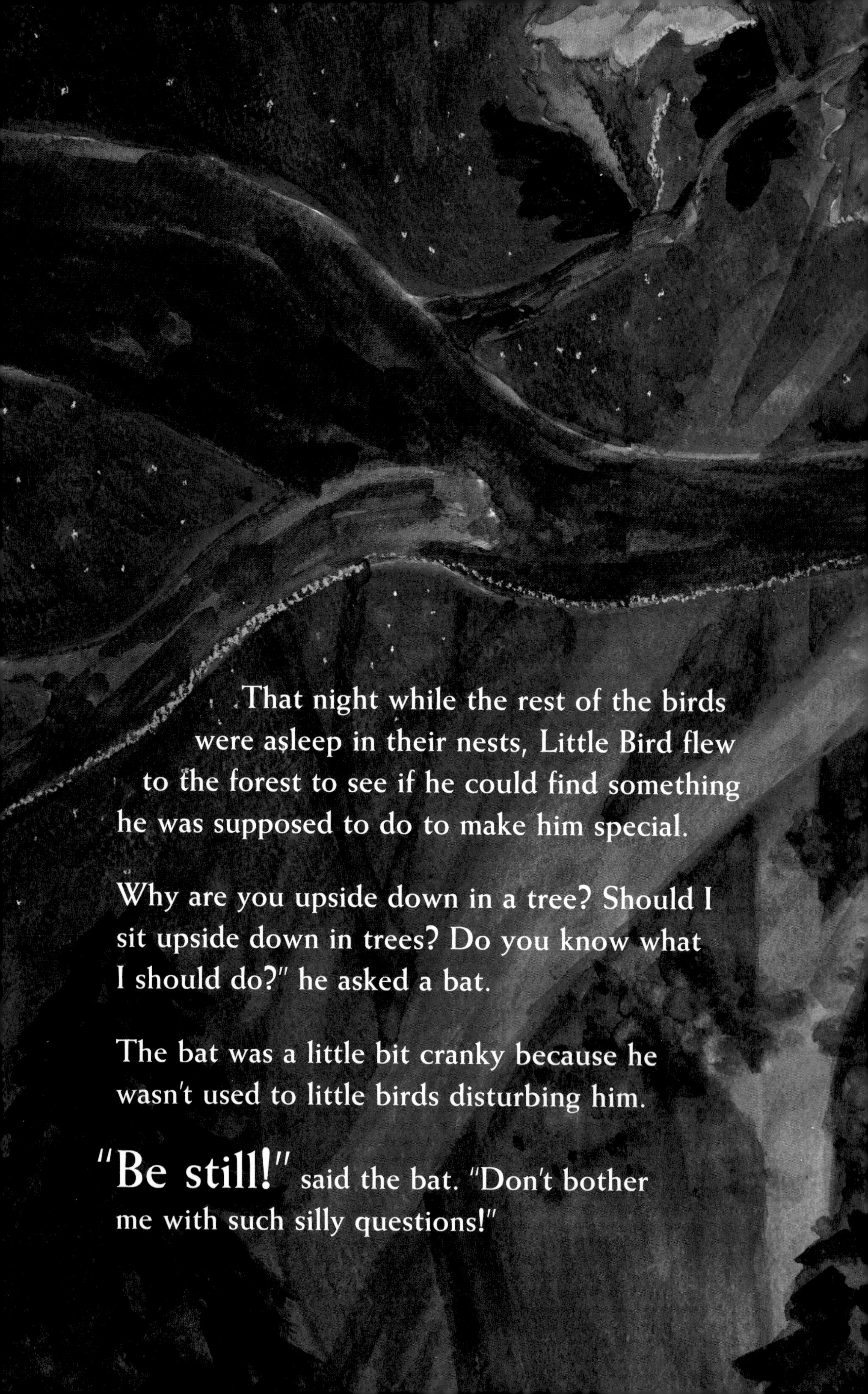

That night while the rest of the birds were asleep in their nests, Little Bird flew to the forest to see if he could find something he was supposed to do to make him special.

Why are you upside down in a tree? Should I sit upside down in trees? Do you know what I should do?" he asked a bat.

The bat was a little bit cranky because he wasn't used to little birds disturbing him.

"**Be still!**" said the bat. "Don't bother me with such silly questions!"

When morning came, Little Bird saw a heron sitting on the dock. Heron was very wise. Surely he could help.

"Oh, Heron, can you help me?" the little bird called out hopefully. "I'm searching everywhere trying to find something to make me special!"

"Be still!"
exclaimed
the heron.

"I asked everyone I've seen, and all they told me was to "Be still", and that was no help!" the little bird said.

Well, it was true that Heron was wise.
He heard the little bird,
alone on his branch, about to give up hope,
and knew what he must do.

"Come here, little bird," called the heron.
Let's sit together on the grass by the shore."

Little Bird and the heron sat on the shore
looking out over the lake.

What you don't understand, my friend,
is that while they may get impatient
with all of your questions, what everyone
is telling you **IS** true. The only way to find
your purpose is to be still. You just need
some help doing it!" smiled the heron.

"There is a place where the answer to your question lies waiting for you to find it. In fact, this place holds all of the answers to all of the questions you may have."

"This is the place I am looking everywhere for!" exclaimed Little Bird. "Can you tell me how to get there?"

"Yes, little bird, I can." said the heron. Now close your eyes and take a deep breath, and become very still..."

Little Bird did as the Heron asked, and became very still. He felt a peaceful feeling starting deep inside his belly.

He took a deep breath. This felt really good. He opened his eyes.

There, reflected in the water was a very handsome little bird staring back at him.

Little Bird still felt warm way deep inside. It spread throughout his body like a smile and he began to hear a voice from within.

"My specialness was here all the time.
My purpose is to be a little bird!
The answer was inside me all along.
I'm important just as I am, and I'm going to be the best little bird I can be!"

"Very good!" said the heron, as he flew away, leaving the little bird to think about what he had learned.

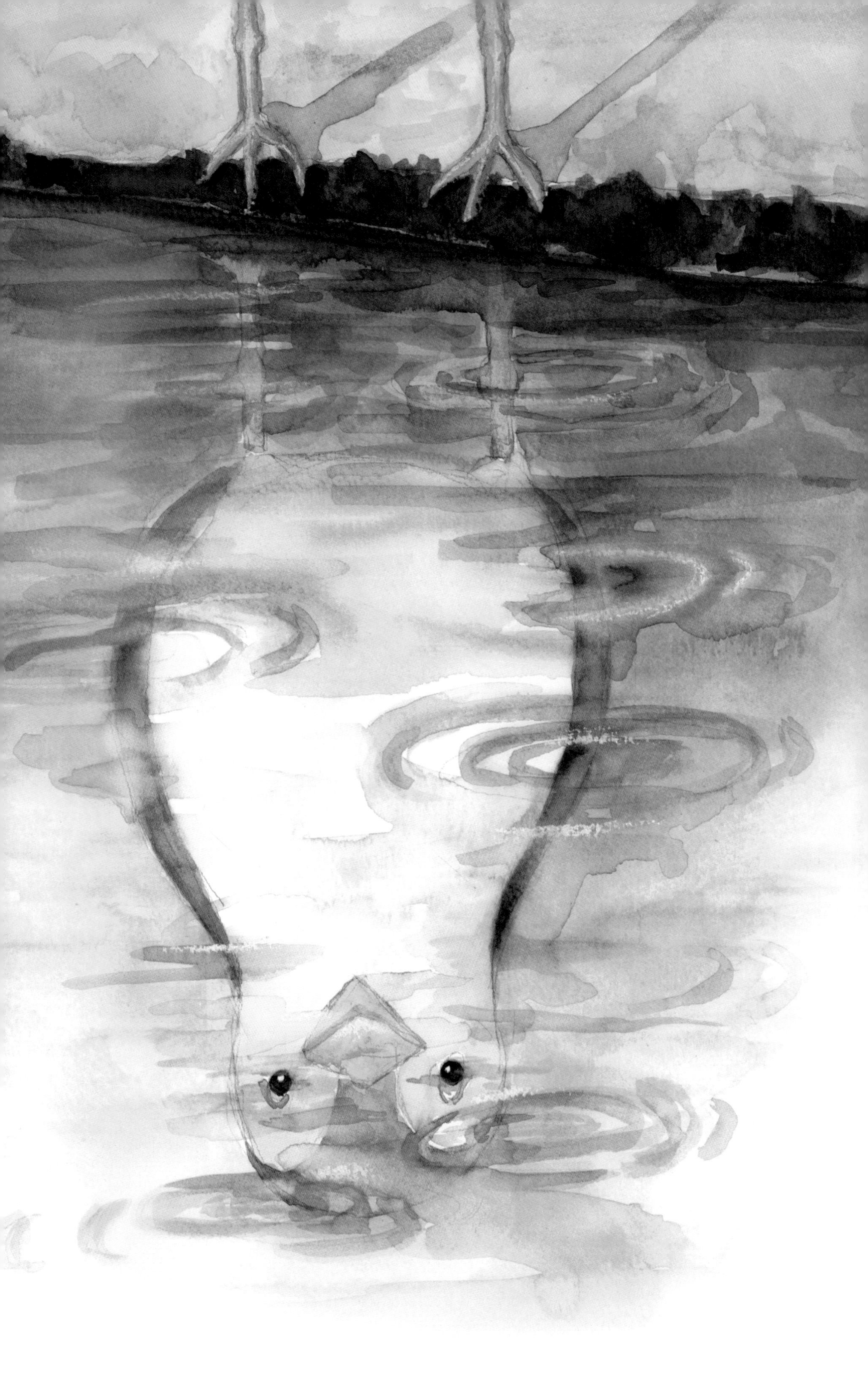

Little Bird still plays and sings and flies around the lake, but he isn't searching for anything.

He knows that all the answers are kept safe deep inside him, and that he only has to become very still to find them there.

You can do it, too. Close your eyes, and breathe right into your belly.

Think about that place inside you that feels bubbly when you're happy. The place that quivers when you're feeling scared. The place in the center of you.

Go there with your mind and be very still.

Now . . . b r e a t h e .

Listen for that little voice inside you.